BIGBen

RACHEL ANDERSON

BIGBen

Illustrated by Jane Ray

Barn Owl Books

To Ben Wharam

BARN OWL BOOKS

157 Fortis Green Road, London, N10 3LX

First Published in Great Britain 1998

This edition Barn Owl Books, 2007
157 Fortis Green Road, London, N10 3LX

Distributed by Frances Lincoln,
4 Torriano Mews, Torriano Avenue, London, NW5 2RZ

ISBN 978 190301570 4

Front cover photograph © Melissa M Gutierrez

Contents

1 Meet Miss Spark

First thing on a normal Wednesday morning, Matthew discovered he had a new teacher.

She breezed in wearing green leather boots tied with red laces, smiling brightly. None of the other teachers wore green boots.

'Wow!' whispered Pritpal who sat next to Matthew. 'Bit of an improvement on old Mr McFee!' Mr McFee always wore the same sad woolly jumper.

The changes began right away. The new teacher beamed round at the class, 'A change is as good as a rest, isn't it?'

First it was the chairs and tables she wanted shifting all about. It made the room seem different.

Next, it was the windows she wanted opening.

'As wide as they'll go, please.'

'But, Miss!' wailed Emily, who began to make herself shiver like a jelly. 'We'll all freeze to death!'

'Nonsense. Nice breath of fresh air never hurt anyone,' said Miss Spark. 'In

fact, the reverse. It helps your brain cells to work properly. And I want you all to concentrate.'

And then she set about changing the way they did their work. Emily made her teeth chatter so loudly that people near her giggled.

Matthew hated changes. Things should stay as they were. Life is easier that way. 'Bet she's on supply,' he muttered. 'Bet she'll only stay one day. She'll be gone by tomorrow.'

But no. By dinner-break they all knew that grey Mr McFee wasn't coming back and bright Miss Spark was staying.

'So you might as well get used to my way of doing things,' she said, beaming round the room like a lighthouse. 'Now then! Please pay attention everyone while I explain the new project you will be starting today.'

Matthew thought about the book he'd begun reading at home. In it, there was a man called Robinson Crusoe who lived on a tropical island, which was exactly where Matthew wanted to be. Alone. Except for Ben of course. He'd always take Ben with him wherever he went because Ben was the best person in the whole world.

Ben was funny and big and had kind brown eyes. He laughed a lot too.
'Yes, you too, Matthew. Pay attention. This is a class project.'

'Mr McFee never made us do class projects,' muttered Matthew.

'Aha! but I expect he did,' said Miss Spark. 'He probably called them something different.'

Miss Spark's project was about the local community, whatever that was.

'It means your neighbourhood, right here where you live and work,' Miss Spark

explained. 'We will be investigating the important day-to-day activities of a range of local citizens, both young and old. We will be finding out what each individual contributes to our community. So you will be choosing someone you know well, perhaps a member of your family or a neighbour, and asking their permission to timetable certain of their regular day's activities. It's going to be simply loads of fun.'

Pritpal, who enjoyed getting involved in any kind of lesson, began scribbling away as though he'd already decided who he'd chosen to study. But Matthew didn't like the sound of it. 'School is school,' he grumbled. 'Family is private.' It wasn't usually a good idea to

let the two get mixed up. For instance, there was the time when Dad brought Ben along to watch the Christmas play. Matthew had been playing an important role as one of the kings, and every time he appeared on stage, Ben had stamped his feet and crowed. This was his way of showing how much he liked something. But most people in the audience didn't know that, and they kept turning round and frowning. Matthew really wanted Ben to be there to enjoy the show but not if it meant strangers staring at him and telling him to sssh. As Miss Spark droned on about how to plan timetables and set out questionnaires, Matthew thought about the plans for the log cabin he was going to build. He and Ben would play at survival on a tropical island. Ben would have to be Robinson Crusoe. Matthew

would be Man Friday, the faithful servant who did everything. Not that it would make much difference to Ben which one he was supposed to be. He was such a good sport, he'd enjoy it either way.

'Our project,' Miss Spark's voice interrupted, 'involves many important skills – design, chronology, interview technique, numbers. And simply loads of practice at data-handling!'

Matthew was sure he heard Miss Spark say 'date handling'. 'What's palm trees got to do with her stupid project?' he whispered to Emily.

But Emily hadn't been listening either. She was flicking paper pellets at Pritpal. She hated seeing other people getting on as though they enjoyed it.

'Search me,' she shrugged.

Pritpal was so bright he could easily fend off pellets at the same time as listening to the teacher, at the same time as planning a timetable.

'Data-handling's her fancy way of talking about facts, what you can do with them. It just means getting lots of info together,' he said.

'Absolutely spot on. Well done!' said Miss Spark. 'We'll end up with a splendid survey covering every aspect of what our community does with its time and how different people's roles interact with each other.'

The end-of-afternoon buzzer went. 'By tomorrow I hope you'll have selected your subjects, ready for my approval.'

Matthew trudged home with a heavy heart. He wouldn't dream of insulting any of his family by asking them to get involved in her project.

⅄ Meet Robinson Crusoe

Ben was waiting and watching at the front window as usual.

'Matt Matty Matt!' he yelled, hugging Matthew tight the minute he got in, as though he was a long-lost brother he hadn't seen for twenty years instead of just a few hours. Not many people got that kind of welcome every time they came home.

After Mum had washed Ben's face and hands, and helped him with his drink, Matthew led him out to the back garden to explain about the log cabin they were going to build. Not that Ben could understand the significance of the measurements, let alone the diagram that Matthew was working out.

'But that's no reason not to keep you fully informed, is it?' Matthew said. Robinson Crusoe and Man Friday hadn't understood each other's language either, but they'd still got on OK. 'And Dad says he'll lend a hand with the construction, as soon as he's got time.' Their Dad often said he'd do things when he had the time. But when he did have time, he was always tired. Just like Mum.

'Yeah. Da Da Dad do it!' agreed
Ben. Matthew folded away the plans and
they had one of their excellent bear-fights
on the grass, rolling and tumbling and
roaring and grunting, until the next-door
neighbour poked her nose over the fence.
'Will you stop making that dreadful
noise!' she said. 'I can't even hear myself
think over here.'

Matthew said, 'It's only pretend fighting. We're not really hurting each other.'

The next-door woman said, 'Well, I've had enough. And in my opinion, that boy should be kept indoors.'

Matthew thought, how *dare* she stop people having a bit of fun?

The next-door woman said, 'I've warned your parents about it before.'

So Matthew took Ben in anyway.

Dad wasn't back. He'd had to go straight to some parents' meeting over at Ben's school on the other side of town.

Poor Ben. Parents' meetings were always bad news.

'What's the meeting for?' Matthew asked.

'Oh, nothing special,' said Mum. 'Just to discuss what will happen when Ben moves on.'

After tea, Matthew got out the Ludo. Ben enjoyed all kinds of board-games, provided Matthew did the counting and made the moves for both of them. He liked shaking the dice in their little plastic beaker, and he never cheated. Ben was older than Matthew so he'd been there since long before Matthew was born, always ready to play whatever Matthew thought up.

In the night, Matthew had a bad dream. It was about a lighthouse and a ferocious tiger he had to save Ben from. He woke up, very scared. But then he heard Ben's noisy snoring from the lower bunk and he felt safe knowing that Ben was there, keeping guard like a faithful watchdog.

3 This is Emily

Matthew wished he could be working out plans on the computer screen for his log cabin instead of having to draw lines and boxes for the project timetable. He was thinking of putting a stockade all around the cabin to keep out the tigers. That would be really fun to do. But you only got a short time on one of the computers

before it was somebody else's turn.
Suddenly, Miss Spark was behind him,
reading over his shoulder.

'Goodness, Matthew!' she said.
'It looks to me as though you've hardly
started. You haven't even
put a name on your
timetable. How can
you plan to interview
someone if you
don't know who
they are?'

'Couldn't think of anyone.'

'Nobody? Really, Matthew. Do you suppose that perhaps you just aren't using your head?'

Matthew shrugged. 'Don't know,' he said. What he meant was, don't care.

Everybody else had chosen their subject. June, for example, was timetabling her newborn baby sister.

'Hey! That's not fair!' Emily complained. 'It'll be easy-peasy for her. She'll be done in half the time it takes the rest of us. Babies don't *do* anything except sleep and cry.'

'Shows how much *you* know about babies,' said June. 'There's *loads* more interesting things in my sister's life than just that. And Miss Spark says even if she doesn't contribute much to the community right now, she will when she grows up. That's because she's got potential.'

Darren had chosen his big brother who was at sixth-form college.

'On the threshold of his life!' said Miss Spark, looking pleased.

Because he was a student, Darren's brother could get up any time he wanted. Then he spent most of the morning sitting around talking ideas and drinking coffee with his mates. That's what Darren said anyhow.

'And in the evening he goes out and plays in a band in his college union,' Darren said.

'Not much timetabling there either,'

said Emily.

Pritpal had chosen his uncle who ran Eezi-Store, the corner shop at the end of School Lane. Mr Singh worked long hours. He kept the shop open, had started the Residents' Association, *and* helped out with the under-twelves' football team. Pritpal hardly had room to keep track of his uncle's day. He had to start a second sheet.

Kim Yen, who hardly ever spoke in class, chose the trainee assistant who date-stamped books at the library. That was because she too wanted to be a librarian when she grew up.

Four people, including Emily, chose Auntie Pat, the school lollipop lady. She wasn't anybody's real aunt but she was everybody's favourite.

'So, Matthew?' said Miss Spark. 'This is supposed to be a group project. And I'm sure you don't want to hold everybody else up. Put on your thinking cap. There must be somebody whose daily life you're specially interested in?'

'Yes', said Matthew. 'Robinson Crusoe.'

'I mean a living person. Come along now, use your brain.'

'Ben,' said Matthew. 'I'm very interested in Ben. He's my favourite person in the whole world.'

'Very well. Sounds promising,' said Miss Spark.

'But he'd never give his permission to be interviewed,'

'Why not?'

Trouble with Miss Spark was that because she was new, she didn't know any of them properly. She didn't know about their families either. At least grey Mr McFee had understood about Ben so he'd never asked difficult questions like this. Matthew couldn't think how to explain to Miss Spark that having a conversation with Ben required quite a special technique. For instance, Ben might easily say, 'Yes,' and actually mean, 'No,' or say, 'No,' and mean, 'Yes,' even to a straightforward question like, 'Ben, do you want some more juice?' So there was no way of knowing how he'd react to an important question like, 'Do you give permission for the timetabling of your daily activities to be used in a school project?

Miss Spark didn't wait for Matthew's answer. She made him write BEN at the top of the timetable sheet. After that she wanted everyone to work in pairs.

'Two heads are always better than one, aren't they, Matthew?' she smiled cheerfully.

It was Matthew's bad luck that he ended up paired with Emily. This was because nobody else in the class would ever choose to work with either of them.

Emily didn't like the arrangement any more than Matthew did.

'It's plain stupid putting your brother in this project. He'll ruin it,' she said with a sneer.

Even if Miss Spark didn't know about Ben, Emily certainly did. Matthew had seen her whispering about Ben in the playground. She'd flapped her arms about and done a silly sideways walk. It wasn't anything like how Ben walked. But

Emily's friends had laughed anyway.

'He's just a dum-dum, isn't he?' Emily said.

'No,' said Matthew who was confused. 'I don't think so.' There were lots of words people used about Ben, but he hadn't heard dum-dum before.

'Course he is. My mum says you have to be careful with kids like your brother. You never know what they might do next. My mum says I must watch out in case he hurts me.'

'Ben would never hurt anybody!' said Matthew. Well, almost never, and only by mistake because he was big and heavy and sometimes he got frustrated if you didn't understand what he was trying to say, whereas people like Emily quite often pinched or crashed into you quite deliberately to hurt.

'He even *looks* dopey,' said Emily.

'No he doesn't. That shows you've never looked at him properly.'

The more Emily said things about Ben, the more Matthew decided he definitely wanted him in the project.

Emily said, '*I'm* going to ask Miss if we ought to include people who are mental.'

Matthew felt himself grow red in the face. Mental was one of the words he definitely knew. He often heard it.

Specially from their next-door neighbour. She was always saying things about Ben, though never directly to his face. It was usually to one of the other neighbours. 'It's high time they got that mental case put away in a home, where someone can take proper care of him. It's a disgrace,' she used to say, though what the disgrace was, Matthew never understood.

Matthew's mum and dad told him that mental was what ignorant people said when they were scared, and that the proper words to say about Ben were 'young adult with profound learning difficulties'. But Matthew thought that was stupid. It was too long, and it didn't describe anything interesting about Ben.

The whole thing made Matthew's

blood boil. 'Ben's not mental!' he said, louder that he meant to, and he grabbed Emily's timetable all about the lollipop lady and he scrumpled it up. 'If my

 brother's mental,' he screamed, 'then so are you!'

Miss Spark stopped smiling and strode over. 'If you can't work like a

civilised human being,' she said with an icy glare, 'then clearly you will have to work on your own.'

She made him go and sit at a table by himself.

All afternoon, Emily made monkey faces and scratched her armpits. Matthew knew she was pretending to be Ben.

He'd show her.

4 Ben and the project

Miss Spark's changes at school were bad enough. But some bad changes were starting at home too. That evening, a stern woman with a briefcase turned up to see Mum and Dad.

'Hello, Matthew,' she said, even though he'd never met her before.

She was very talkative so Matthew

stayed outside with Ben and got going on the school project.

'We'll do some work on the cabin after this, OK?' He was pleased with the way he'd decided to set out the question sheets. 'Right, Ben are you listening? It's quite easy. I just ask you a few questions and then I fill in the boxes with the answers. The first section we'll do is about food, how people shop, what they eat, why they like certain things.'

'Yeah,' said Ben.

They'd had a class discussion about food preferences and discovered, for example, that Darren's brother ate chips for almost every meal while Pritpal's uncle, Mr Singh, ate chapattis and dahl, and although Mr Singh had occasionally eaten chips, Darren's brother had never tried a chapatti.

Ben liked eating all sorts of things. Paper was his latest favourite; used envelopes, biscuit wrappers, or little strips he tore off the *Evening News*. It wasn't so much the taste he seemed to like as the feel of it in his mouth. Obviously this wasn't the kind of thing Miss Spark would want in his project, so Matthew wrote, *Person questioned prefers healthy, balanced diet, fish fingers, sausages and lots of vegetables. Not too much chocolate.*

Then he skipped on to PREFERRED TELEVISION VIEWING.

This was easy. Ben's favourite programme had to be the weather forecast. He'd wave his fist and say,

'Sshhh! Very important! Quiet now. Quiet!' Dad said he thought it was because  Ben liked the theme tune.

Filling in SPORT AND RECREATION was more difficult. Ben didn't collect stamps or build model aeroplanes, didn't belong to any clubs or play football. Matthew couldn't think that Ben had any recreations whatever. In fact, apart from going to school and playing at bears and Robinson Crusoe, Ben didn't do a lot.

In class discussion, Miss Spark mentioned the invisible members of society, like night nurses, milkmen, who did important jobs to serve the community but who you didn't often see. Matthew wondered if Ben counted as an invisible member of society.

Matthew looked through what he'd written so far. He was disappointed. Even when he'd filled in the address, and Ben's birthday, and what time Ben left for school, and when he got back, it didn't add up to much. Miss Spark was bound to complain that there wasn't enough. Matthew decided to put in a load of invented stuff, about Ben belonging to Judo club, and playing in a rock band like Darren's brother.

Ben was growing restless, stomping round the garden with a hungry look in

his eyes.

'I'll go and see if tea's ready yet, Ben,' Matthew said.

But the woman with the briefcase was still there, still talking.

Mum said, 'We're nearly through. Tea in about ten minutes, OK?'

Matthew had only left Ben on his own for a few moments. When he got back, Ben was sitting, very quietly, munching. There were little strips of paper all over the grass and quite a lot in Ben's mouth.

'Oh, Ben! My project!' There was no point being cross, but Matthew couldn't stop himself. He was furious. 'Look at it! You've ruined it!' he yelled. 'How could you do that when it's about you? Aren't you proud to be part of my project? Come on, open up!' The only way to get

something out of Ben's mouth was to pinch his nostrils.

Ben roared. Dad came striding out. 'For heaven's sake, you lads. What on earth's going on?'

'Look what he's done!' Matthew wailed.

Ben drummed his heels on the ground.

'Calm down, both of you, at once!' Dad said.

'That's my homework! It's our class project. But nothing's ever safe with *him* around!'

'Look, it'll be alright. He hasn't eaten it all.' Dad smoothed out some of the bits and Matthew suddenly wondered, did his parents know how he used to wish that Ben wasn't always here, taking up all their time? Did they know that he wished he had a bit more of Dad and Mum to himself?

'But how am I going to tell Miss Spark?' he said.

'Tell the truth. A pinch of truth's worth ten pounds of fibs.'

Matthew realised his Dad didn't understand the first thing about school. How could he possibly tell anyone that his big brother had eaten his part of the class project? If Emily got to hear of it she'd laugh like a drain.

5 Forward to the future

Ages after their normal teatime, the talkative woman finally gathered up her papers and left. Matthew wondered what was going on. He knew it must be something to do with Ben. Most things were. Sometimes it was the social worker's visit. Or it was an appointment at the hearing clinic. Or Ben's feet had grown and he had to be remeasured for the boots which were so special you couldn't just buy them in the shoe-shop in the High Street. Or he was going into hospital to have his teeth seen to because he couldn't pop along to the dentist in the holidays like Matthew did. Even for a small filling, he had to have a general anaesthetic.

But, this time, it wasn't any of the usual things. It was something much more serious. Mum said, 'It's about when Ben moves on. We've been discussing it with Mrs Rawlings.'

'Moves on? What d'you mean?'

'When he leaves school.'

'Oh that,' said Matthew, without thinking too much about it because everybody has to leave school eventually.

But then Mum said, 'She thinks she's found us the ideal place. So we're going over to visit the unit on Saturday. D'you want to come too? It'll be nice if you do. It's a couple of hours' drive, so we'll have to make an early start.'

'Two hours' drive every morning? You can't make Ben do that! He'd be completely knackered!' Ben got car-sick on even quite short car journeys.

Mum said, quite casually, 'Oh no, it won't be every morning. Only once a week. The centre is fully residential. He'll be a boarder there.'

Matthew was shocked. 'You mean he'd have to *sleep* somewhere different?' Ben had never slept away from home in his life, except when they went on holiday to the seaside, but at least they were all together. Then Matthew wondered, was it actually *his* fault that they were thinking that Ben had to go away? Was it because he'd lost his temper with him when he ate the project?

He said, 'You mustn't do this to him. No way.' He turned to his father. 'Dad, you can't get rid of him!'

'Nobody's getting rid of anybody,' said Dad. 'Whatever gave you that idea?'

'Sending him away. Moving him on. It's the same thing. I suppose it's because that horrid woman next door's been saying nasty things again. You shouldn't take any notice.'

'Matthew, my old mate, of course it's not because of that. We've got to think about Ben's long-term future.'

Matthew thought, and what about me? He said, 'You know it'll ruin my project if he's not here.'

'Ben's a big boy now. He's nearly a man.'

'No he's not! He can't be.' Matthew didn't want his brother to be a man. That was scary. He wanted his brother to stay as he was. 'You're just like Miss Spark. Why do you grown-ups have to keep changing things just when they seem to be all right?'

Mum said, 'Really Matthew. Don't be difficult. Ben's growing up. You're both growing up.'

'That's no reason for sending him off to some disabled prison place,' said

Matthew.

'Prison?' said Dad, laughing. 'Why d'you call it that? It's a Special Needs Sixteen-Plus Unit, which means that you have to be over sixteen to go there.' Ben was nearly seventeen.

Mum said, 'Obviously, we're a bit anxious. But Ben definitely wants to give it his best shot, don't you?'

Ben was sitting behind the sofa, scowling.

'Doesn't look like it to me,' said Matthew and he stormed up to his room without even touching his fish fingers.

He read some of *Robinson Crusoe* for a while. But when he heard Mum coming up with Ben, he switched out the lights, slid *Robinson Crusoe* under his pillow, and pretended to be asleep. He listened to the sounds of Mum helping Ben get into his pyjamas.

'There we go then, my lad,' Mum was saying quietly. 'Well done. Good boy.'

Good *boy*? Downstairs, Dad had said how Ben was nearly a man. Now Mum was calling him a good boy. They obviously couldn't make up their own mind what he was.

'Night-night-night, Matty-matt!' Ben started crowing.

'Sssh, Ben,' said Mum. 'Don't wake him.'

Matthew heard Mum help Ben on to the lower bunk. 'No, not that way, you old silly-billy,' she whispered.'Put your head here, on the pillow.' When Ben was tired, he could forget even the simplest thing,

like how to get into bed the right way.

Matthew heard the stiff crackle of the plastic undersheet as Ben lay down, then the noisy goodnight kisses.

Who would kiss Ben goodnight if he was sent away? And who would take care of Matthew if he got scared of the dark?

6 Meet Matthew on his own.

Before Mum set off with Dad and Ben to visit the unit, she got loads of food ready for Matthew, far more than he could eat in half a day.

'Now are you *quite* sure you'll be all right?' she kept saying as though Matthew hadn't ever had to be left on his own before.

'Course I will,' said Matthew. 'Been taking care of myself for years, haven't I?' Taken care of Ben too, quite often. So why did Mum start worrying all of a sudden?

But once they'd left, Matthew felt miserable. He didn't want to eat anything, didn't want to watch telly, didn't want to get on with the class project. And he certainly didn't want to do any more to the log cabin. There wasn't any point in finishing it now, not if Ben wasn't going to be around much longer.

Matthew sat under the washing-line and thought sad thoughts until the next-door neighbour poked her head over the fence and said, 'Everything all right, sonny?'

'Yes,' he said grumpily, 'Course it is.'

'Such a shame about your poor brother,' she said. 'Still, at least your parents have got you.'

'They've still got both of us,' said Matthew and he ran indoors so he wouldn't have to go on listening to her.

Mum and Dad were excited when they got back.

'Ben's going for a month's trial period,' Mum said. 'Aren't you, Ben? And if that goes all right, they'll offer him a permanent place.'

Mum explained the plans clearly to Ben lots of times and she bought him his own tartan suitcase. It seemed to Matthew that Ben still hadn't a clue what the new suitcase was for or what was about to happen to him. But he told himself he mustn't worry about his brother when he'd got troubles enough of his own.

At school, Miss Spark was harrassing everybody to hurry up and hand in their project work. Every morning, Matthew had to pretend he'd forgotten to bring it in. How was he going to finish it if Ben wasn't living at home?

'By next week then,' said Miss Spark sternly. 'At the very latest.'

On Ben's last night at home, Mum

packed his case. Ben watched as his clothes, a pair of new pyjamas, a new toothbrush and toothpaste in a new toilet-bag, all went in.

Matthew watched too. He said, 'He ought to take something special with him. So he'll feel safe. So he won't forget us.'

Mum said, 'Good idea, Matt. Can you choose something you know he likes?'

'He ought to choose himself.' Matthew handed Ben a little photo in a gold frame of them both standing in the waves on holiday last year.

But Ben shook his head. 'Nah!'

'What about your teddy then.'

Ben shook his head again.

'You're right. You're too old for teddies.' Matthew offered him his own very best music tape, then his football supporters' scarf. Ben didn't want any of them.

'Well, what *do* you want?'

'Camping,' said Ben with a grin and he bounded across the bedroom, rummaged under Matthew's pillow, and pulled out the copy of *Robinson Crusoe*.

'Oh,' said Matthew. ' All right. But

bring it back. I haven't finished it yet.'

Mum clicked shut the case. 'I'll never understand how you tick, Ben,' she said with a laugh.

'Why ever have

you got to take Matt's story book when you can't even read?'

That first Monday evening when Ben wasn't there was terrible. The house seemed as quiet as a grave. At tea-time, Mum and Dad hardly spoke at all. Going up to bed was eerie. Lying in bed with no snoring from the bottom bunk was lonely.

Matthew kept wondering, was Ben feeling lonely too? It must be worse for him, in a strange bed, in a strange room, not understanding why he'd been banished like Robinson Crusoe.

Quite late, Dad came up to say goodnight. He put his arms out for a cuddle. Matthew wriggled away.

'Yes I know, Matthew, old son. It's going to be tough for us all, getting used to it. Mum and I aren't even sure how it's going to work out. But trust us. We're trying to do what's best for everybody. And that includes you.'

Matthew felt bad. He wished there was something he could do to put everything back the way it used to be before the changes began. He felt like blaming it all on Miss Spark.

7 Meet Kim Yen

'Dad, I wish he hadn't gone. I miss him too much,' he said, and began to cry. This time, when Dad reached out his arms, Matthew let himself be drawn into a hug. He sobbed for a long time while Dad stroked his head.

'Shall I read to you?' Dad asked at last. He hadn't read aloud to Matthew for ages.

Matthew sniffed. 'You can't. Ben's taken *Robinson Crusoe* with him.'

'Then let's have something different,' said Dad. He looked along the shelf and chose a book. 'Ah, this one looks fun,'

Even when you could read to yourself quite well, it was better being read aloud to, especially by Dad. He put on a different voice for each of the characters.

Next morning, Matthew knew what he could do to make things feel a bit better at school. He could start telling the truth.

He could explain to Miss Spark why he hadn't finished his project work. He didn't want to pass the blame to Ben, but he wanted Miss Spark to know what sort of a person Ben was.

After Register he went up to her desk, took a deep breath and said it very quickly before he could change his mind.

At first, Miss Spark looked as though she didn't believe a single word of it.

'But,' Matthew went on quickly, 'it wasn't his fault he ate it. It was all mine. I left it where he could reach it.'

People in the front row started listening. Matthew thought he heard a snigger. But suddenly he didn't care if people laughed.

'You see, my brother is disabled. He has profound learning difficulties. This means that he can't do all the things that other people do. He can't even go out by himself. He never gets the chances we get with football and clubs and stuff.'

At first, Matthew felt shy speaking about his brother, but the more he said, the stronger he felt.

'Another reason I haven't finished the project is that my brother's just moved away from home for the first time in his life, which is actually a very brave thing to have to do.'

Matthew glanced around the classroom. They were all listening to him, especially Miss Spark. She wasn't smiling but she nodded to him to carry on.

'And because Ben can't speak properly, he may not be able to tell me what he'll be up to. But just because he's disabled and doesn't seem to be doing anything useful that fills up a big timetable, and just because he'll need to be looked after for the rest of his life, doesn't mean that he doesn't count. My brother's still part of the community.'

Matthew suddenly ran out of steam. He sat down feeling red in the face. He waited for Emily to start laughing like a drain.

Instead, Miss Spark smiled and said, 'Why, Matthew, I didn't know you had it in you! That was a magnificent effort. A clear, well thought-out, beautifully expressed oral presentation. This definitely deserves a round of applause from everybody.' Matthew went even redder as the whole class clapped.

At the end of the lesson, Miss Spark asked Matthew to stay behind. 'Matthew, what you told the class will count towards your project, and perhaps you can give us an update later.'

At break-time, Kim Yen sidled up to Matthew in the playground. He tried to edge out of her way. But she followed.

'Yes?' he hissed.

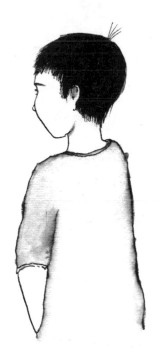

'It was brilliant,' she whispered, so quietly that Matthew could hardly hear. 'To say all that in class. I wouldn't have dared. My aunty's like your brother, only my aunty eats soap. She lives with us. We all love her, but my parents feel sad for her too. Other people never really understand do they, even when they pretend to? And when your brother came to the school play, that was brave too.' Then Kim Yen turned and ran away.

Matthew was surprised. Kim Yen always looked so perfect. You'd never have imagined there was someone with learning difficulties in her family.

After school, something else rather unusual happened. Dad got in from work early and said, 'Got time for a game of football before tea, Matthew?'

They wandered up to the playing field and kicked the ball about for a while till some other kids came and joined in. Mr Singh was there too.

'I see your lad's quite promising,' he said to Dad. 'Has he thought of joining our under-twelves' team?'

And the next evening, something else unusual happened. Mum, Dad and Matthew went out to see a film at the cinema. The evening after, Mum came up the garden to see how the log cabin was getting on, and the two of them played a game of Ludo which was quite different from playing it with Ben. Mum also

taught Matthew a card trick.

Matthew said, 'I didn't even know you knew how to play cards!

On Friday afternoon, instead of Ben at the window watching out for Matthew to come home, it was Matthew who was waiting anxiously for big Ben.

8 Meet Ben, the student

Ben came steaming down the steps of the minibus. He was grinning all round. The bus escort handed out his smart tartan case. Once he was indoors, Ben tipped everything on to the floor and scrabbled through it. He pulled out a clay mug he'd made and gave it to Matthew, and a sunflower seed he'd planted for Mum. He

Ben's Timetable (summer term)

DAY	a.m		p.m	
Mon.				
Tues.				
Weds.				
Thurs.				
Fri.				
Notes				

also had his own weekly timetable, stuck on to a piece of card, with little pictures to remind him what he'd be doing each day.

'Hey, Ben!' said Matthew. 'This is ace! You're doing loads of stuff, aren't you? Can I copy some of it for my class project?'

Every day, from Monday till Friday,

students at the unit were busy with important things.

'Skills,' said Ben, nodding. 'Big skills.'

On his timetable, there was a picture of a flower to show when he helped with the unit's gardening, a wooden spoon to show when it was his turn for helping with the baking, a football to remind him when it was time for sport. He'd also be finding out about using the telephone, sending a postcard, making his own bed, and lots of other things.

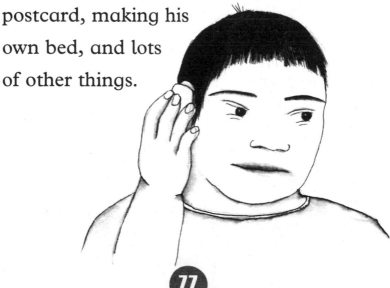

Matthew could see that being at a sixteen-plus unit was a million times more interesting than pretending to be marooned on a desert island like Robinson Crusoe and having to watch your brother building a hut out of old logs.

It was probably quite tiring too, because Ben slept most of the weekend, just like Darren said *his* big brother did.

And after that, the family got so used to Ben being away all week, then back for the weekends, that it seemed quite normal.

A few weeks later, the unit was holding its spring open day so Ben wouldn't be coming home. Matthew felt sorry for him having to stay away all weekend. On Saturday, he and Mum and Dad got up early and drove over there instead. It was a long way. Matthew counted the bridges on the motorway and ate slices of apple to stop himself feeling car-sick.

The open day was a bit like a grand garden party. Some of the mothers were even wearing smart hats. Matthew was surprised that it was the students who were mostly in charge of the events.

Two of them, wearing armbands, which said, PARKING ATTENDANT, directed the cars about on the football field and told Matthew's dad exactly where to put his car. Other students welcomed visitors in as they arrived at the main building. It was more students who pointed out the way to reach the different workshops, and the garden centre, and the gymnasium and sports complex.

At first they couldn't find Ben anywhere. Mum began to worry. 'Oh dear, I do hope he's not got himself in a muddle because of us coming to visit.'

When Ben got excited about birthdays or Christmas, he often got himself into a muddle. Matthew thought that Ben was probably hiding and was going to jump out at them.

Dad said, 'Don't be such a pair of sillies. I'm sure we'll find him soon enough. He's probably busy.'

It turned out that Ben was one of the guides in charge at the pool.

He was wearing blue swimming

trunks, a whistle on a string round his neck, and a black singlet which said,

TRAINEE LIFEGUARD. He looked very proud and serious walking round the pool making sure that none of the visitors fell in. Matthew realised he'd completely forgotten to mention on his project timetable anything about Ben enjoying swimming. Dad had taught them both to swim one summer when they went on holiday to the seaside.

'Life-saving, life,' said Ben.

One of the members of staff explained that several of the students were doing a life-saving course, and they'd be doing a test before the end of term.

'Certificate,' Ben agreed.

The water in the pool was a lovely blue colour, cool and inviting. Matthew went over to the edge to take a closer look and check how deep it was. But Ben immediately blew sharply on his whistle and waved his arm. All visitors, Matthew included, were supposed to stay behind the safety barrier.

Matthew stepped back at once, feeling embarrassed. Ben patted him on the shoulder and nodded as though to say he was sorry he'd had to be firm, but he had a job to do and rules were rules.

Later, when Ben was dressed again, they met him in the training canteen where teas and snacks were being prepared and served by the students, who wore proper chefs' white uniforms. After having some scones and sandwiches, Matthew's mum and dad bought a packet of flap-jacks to take home, which Ben had helped bake.

When it was time to leave, Ben went with them as far as the main entrance gates. They hugged and said goodbye. Mum hugged the longest of all and Matthew thought she was definitely sniffing a bit as they walked back to the car.

He took her hand and held it firmly. He held his dad's hand on the other side. He knew they might go on feeling a little bit sad about their eldest son for the rest of their lives, like Kim Yen said happened in her family.

'At least we know that he's really happy here, don't we?' Matthew said, and as they drove away, he waved out of the back window. But Ben was so busy galloping across the grass to catch up with two other young men that he hardly even noticed. He was definitely changing. He looked practically grown-up.

★　　★　　★

That night, on the top bunk, Matthew made a wish.

'When I grow up, I hope I'll be able to go away to college, just like my big brother.'

About the Author

Rachel Anderson was born in 1943. She has worked in radio and journalism. Rachel has written four books for adults and fifty-five for young readers, she lives in Norfolk with her husband and has several grandchildren and two goldfish.

This book draws extensively on the experiences that Rachel has had with children with disabilities, and demonstrates her commitment to them.

MIND THE DOOR!

by Steve Skidmore and Steve Barlow
Illustrated by Tony Ross

Mr O'Taur is a brilliant caretaker. He keeps the school spotless. He runs the gym club. He even wears a trendy nose-ring! Andy thinks Mr O'Taur is great.

Perce isn't so sure. He seems a bit of a bully to her. Her quest for the truth leads Perce, Andy, Well'ard and Eddie Johnson into a labyrinth of mysteries, dangers and dark deeds.

A madcap retelling of the Minotaur myth by 'The Two Steves'.

"A pair of authors who have their finger on the pulse of junior humour."

The Times Literary Supplement

£4.99

Others in the Mad Myth Series

– meet all your favourite characters from the Greek myths –

STONE ME!

A TOUCH OF WIND!

DON'T LOOK BACK!

MUST FLY!

ARABEL'S RAVEN

by Joan Aiken
Illustrated by Quentin Blake

This is the first of many wonderful stories about Arabel and her pet raven Mortimer.

When Arabel's dad brings a wet raven home for his daughter it is love at first sight. 'His name is Mortimer' she announced, 'and Mortimer has found a home.'

Mr and Mrs Jones find the bad tempered raven rather a difficult guest but Arabel insists that he stay. A series of thefts and a robber squirrel are only two of the dramas in this delightful tale of chaos and mayhem.

Mortimer and Arabel find their way straight into our hearts and Quentin Blake's enchanting drawings are to die for.

£3.99

Others stories in the series

MORTIMER'S BREAD BIN

THE SPIRAL STAIR

MORTIMER AND THE ESCAPED
BLACK MAMBA

MORTIMER AND THE SWORD
EXCALIBUR

Order online at
www.franceslincoln.com

If you've enjoyed this book, you can find
more great titles from Barn Owl at

www.barnowlbooks.com